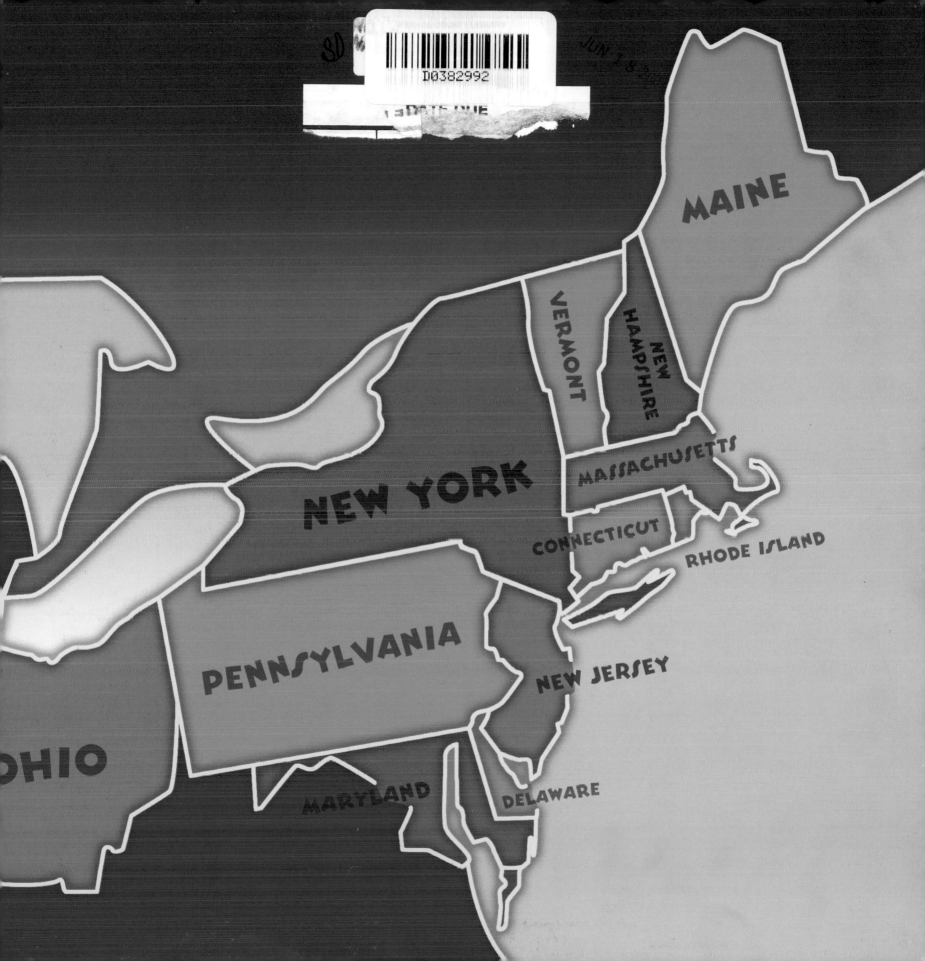

MAINE

VERMONT

NEW
HAMPSHIRE

NEW YORK

MASSACHUSETTS

CONNECTICUT

RHODE ISLAND

PENNSYLVANIA

NEW JERSEY

OHIO

MARYLAND

DELAWARE

Text copyright © 2006 by Miles Backer

Pictures copyright © 2006 by Chuck Nitzberg

CIP Data is available.

Published in the United States 2006 by

🍎 Blue Apple Books

P.O. Box 1380, Maplewood, N.J. 07040

www.blueapplebooks.com

Distributed in the U.S. by Chronicle Books

First Edition

Printed in China

ISBN 10: 1-59354-162-7

ISBN 13: 978-1-59354-162-0

1 3 5 7 9 10 8 6 4 2

TRAVELS with CHARLIE

Travelin' the Northeast

Miles Backer

Illustrated by **Chuck Nitzberg**

 BLUE APPLE BOOKS

You'll spy Pea Patch Island
and West Quoddy Light.
You'll find a jazz festival
on a warm summer night.

You'll see Mystic Seaport.
You'll find Menlo Park,
where Thomas A. Edison
lit up the dark.

You'll spot Blow-Me-Down Bridge.

You'll see Plimoth Plantation
and the Liberty Bell,
which rang in a new nation.

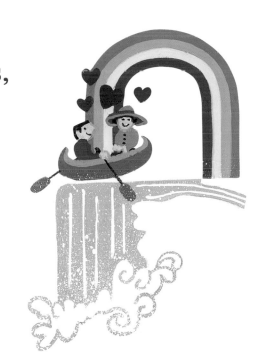

You'll see Assateague ponies,
a monster named Champ,
Niagara Falls,
and a huge rubber stamp.

Just follow Charlie
wherever he goes.
He's in the Northeast,
but just where, who knows?

Connecticut

STATE CAPITAL
HARTFORD

STATE FLAG

DID YOU KNOW...

- Each year on April 27 Ridgefield residents and military buffs re-create the 1777 battle of Ridgefield.

- The Hartford *Courant* is the oldest continuously published newspaper in the U.S.

- P. T. Barnum, who founded the circus that eventually became the Ringling Brothers and Barnum & Bailey Circus, was born in Bethel, CT, on July 5, 1810. The Barnum Museum now stands in Bridgeport, CT, and features exhibits on Barnum's life and also on 19th-century Bridgeport.

- Mystic Seaport is a re-creation of a 19th-century seaport consisting of more than 60 original buildings that were transported to a 37-acre site in Mystic, CT. Mystic Seaport boasts a large collection of rare sailing ships and boats, including the only surviving wooden sailing whaler.

Where's Mystic Seaport
where tall ships are found?
Where's the Barnum Museum?
Where's Long Island Sound?

Where's Yale University,
the third in the land?
Where's Ridgefield,
where Patriots once took a stand?

Where's Charlie?

WADSWORTH ATHENEUM
MUSEUM OF ART

LITCHFIELD
HILLS

ANTIQUES

Hartford

DINOSAUR
STATE PARK

CONNECTICUT RIVER

DINOSAUR X-ING

YALE
UNIVERSITY

FOXWOODS
CASINO

Ledyard

Mystic

MYSTIC
SEAPORT

Ridgefield

New Haven

P. T.
BARNUM
MUSEUM

Bridgeport

LONG ISLAND SOUND

AMISTAD

Delaware

THE FiRST STATE

DiD You Know...

- Winterthur, the estate of Henry du Pont, is situated on 982 acres of land and has its own post office and fire station.

- Dr. Henry Heimlich, inventor of the Heimlich Maneuver, was born on February 3, 1920, in Wilmington, DE. The Heimlich Maneuver has saved over 50,000 Americans from choking or drowning.

- In 1802, Eleuthère Irénée du Pont started a gunpowder mill on the Brandywine Creek near Wilmington. Since then, the DuPont company has become the second largest chemical company in the world.

- The Battle of Cooch's Bridge was fought on September 3, 1777, near Wilmington, DE. It was the only Revolutionary War battle fought in the state of Delaware and was also the first time the Stars and Stripes were flown during battle.

Find Pea Patch Island
and Fort Delaware.
Where's Winterthur?
Be sure to go there!

Find Dover to see
the John Dickinson Plantation.
Find the Indian River
Life-Saving Station.

Where's Charlie?

COOCH'S BRIDGE

WINTERTHUR

Wilmington

PEA PATCH ISLAND

FORT DELAWARE

ENCHANTED WOODS

Dover

JOHN DICKINSON PLANTATION

KILLENS POND STATE PARK

REHOBOTH BEACH

ZWAANENDAEL MUSEUM

INDIAN RIVER LIFE-SAVING STATION

GREAT CYPRESS SWAMP

Maine

THE PINE TREE STATE

STATE CAPITAL
AUGUSTA

STATE FLAG

DID YOU KNOW . . .

- Maine is the only state with a one-syllable name.

- More than 57,000,000 pounds of lobster were harvested in 2000.

- Rockland is the "lobster capital of the world."

- Maine has some 29,000 moose.

- Eastport, ME, is the easternmost city in the United States. West Quoddy Head is the easternmost point in the United States.

- Maine has 63 lighthouses spread out over 5,000 miles of coastline.

Where's a lobster in Rockland?

Where's Moosehead Lake?

Where is the house
that's called "Wedding Cake"?

Where's Old Orchard Beach?

Where's Baxter State Park?

Where's the West Quoddy Light
to help ships in the dark?

Where's Charlie?

WORLD'S LARGEST COFFEE POT

BAXTER STATE PARK

MOOSEHEAD LAKE

MT. KITAHDIN

Island Falls

WEST QUODDY LIGHTHOUSE

Bangor

ROCKLAND LOBSTER FESTIVAL

SUGAR LOAF SKI RESORT

Farmington

KENNEBEC RIVER

Augusta

Rockland

WEDDING CAKE HOUSE

Kennebunkport

Portland

OLD ORCHARD BEACH

Maryland

THE OLD LINE STATE

STATE CAPITAL

ANNAPOLIS

STATE FLAG

DID YOU KNOW...

- George Herman Ruth, Jr., better known as Babe Ruth, was born in Baltimore, MD, on February 6, 1895.

- Maryland's official sport is jousting! Every year there are several tournaments.

- On October 10, 1845, the United States Naval Academy was founded in Annapolis, MD.

- The skipjack is the official state boat of Maryland. Skipjacks are working sailboats, used to dredge oysters from the floor of the Chesapeake Bay.

Where is a skipjack

on Chesapeake Bay?

Where's Assateague Island

where wild ponies play?

Where's Fort McHenry,

where Francis Scott Key

wrote the "Star Spangled Banner."

"Oh, say can you see!"

Where's Charlie?

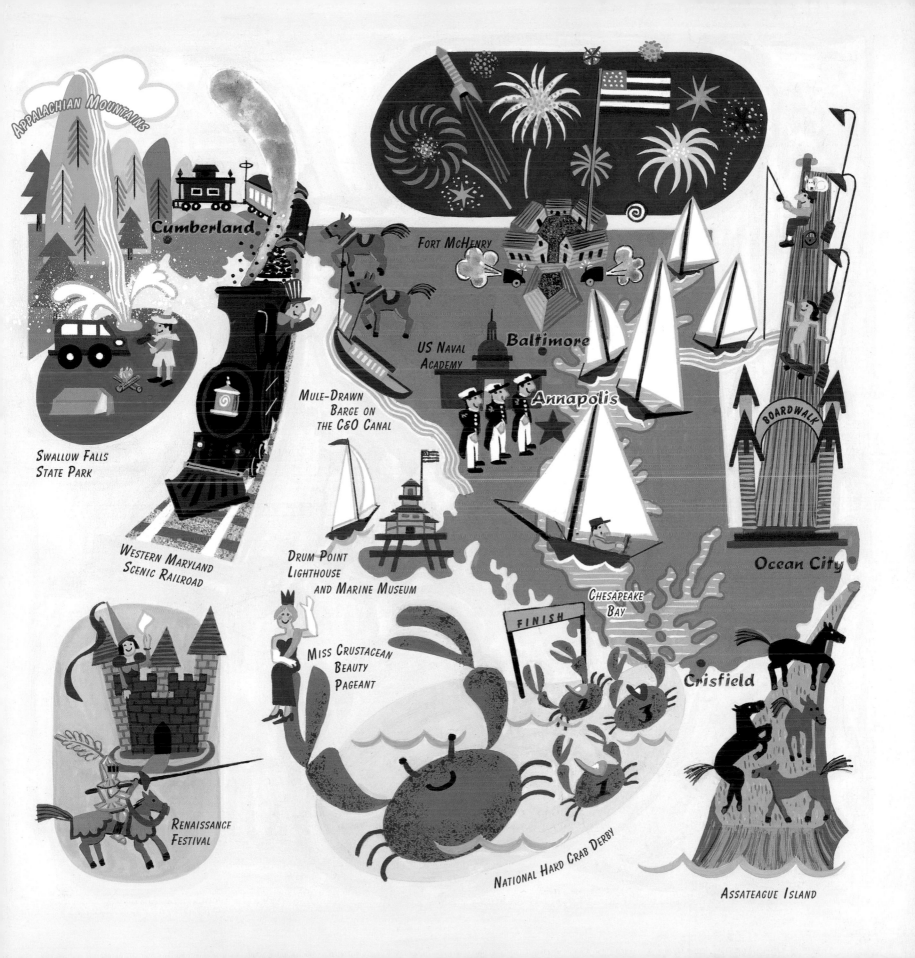

Appalachian Mountains

Cumberland

Swallow Falls
State Park

Western Maryland
Scenic Railroad

Mule-Drawn
Barge on
the C&O Canal

Drum Point
Lighthouse
and Marine Museum

Fort McHenry

US Naval
Academy

Baltimore

Annapolis

BOARDWALK

Ocean City

Chesapeake
Bay

Renaissance
Festival

Miss Crustacean
Beauty
Pageant

FINISH

Crisfield

National Hard Crab Derby

Assateague Island

Massachusetts

THE BAY STATE

STATE CAPITAL
BOSTON

STATE FLAG

DID YOU KNOW...

- About 32 percent of the nation's cranberries are grown in Massachusetts. Cranberries are grown in bogs and require an inch of water a week to grow.

- Harvard was the first university established in the U.S.

- Nantucket Island was once the whaling capital of the world.

- The *U.S.S. Constitution*, known as "Old Ironsides," is the oldest commissioned ship in the world that is still afloat. Commissioned in 1797, this wooden-hulled, three-masted frigate is considered a "ship of state" and is docked in Boston.

Where's music at Tanglewood?

Where's Old Ironsides?

Where's Old Sturbridge Village?

Where did Paul Revere ride?

Where are cranberry bogs?

Where's Plimoth Plantation?

Where's the birthplace of Adams,

who helped found our nation?

Where's Charlie?

WILLIAMSTOWN
THEATER

PIONEER VALLEY
MOHAWK TRAIL

HOUSE OF THE SEVEN GABLES

OLD
IRONSIDES

Williamstown

TANGLEWOOD

BASKETBALL
HALL OF FAME

Salem

Lexington

Boston

Quincy

PLIMOTH PLANTATION

Springfield

Sturbridge
Village

Adams' House

Provincetown

Berkshire
Mountains

Plymouth

CAPE COD

CRANBERRY BOGS

MARTHA'S VINEYARD

NANTUCKET

New Hampshire

THE GRANITE STATE

Where's the world's largest barrel?

Where's Blow-Me-Down Bridge?

Where's Ruggle's Mine?

Where's Franconia Ridge?

Where's Hanover, which

Daniel Webster called home?

Where's Concord, where you'll

find the capital's dome?

Where's Charlie?

MT. WASHINGTON

COG RAILROAD

Franconia Ridge

DANIEL WEBSTER FARM HOUSE

Hanover

NEW HAMPSHIRE SNOW MOBILE MUSEUM

BLOW-ME-DOWN BRIDGE

Grafton

Concord

Portsmouth

RUGGLE'S MINE

New Jersey

THE GARDEN STATE

Where's Atlantic City?
Look on this map
for the Hermitage in Ho-Ho-Kus
and the Delaware Gap.

Find where Thomas A. Edison
once made his mark
by inventing the lightbulb
in Menlo Park.

Where's Charlie?

KITTATINNY MOUNTAINS

DELAWARE WATER GAP

HO-HO-KUS HERMITAGE

Newark

SANDY HOOK TWIN LIGHTS LIGHTHOUSE

EDISON MUSEUM

Menlo Park

FIRST DRIVE-IN MOVIE

Princeton

Trenton

WARREN COUNTY HOT AIR BALLOON FESTIVAL

JERSEY TOMATO FESTIVAL

Camden

Atlantic City

CASINO

WALT WHITMAN HOUSE

BOARDWALK

STEEL PIER

Cape May

New York

THE EMPIRE STATE

Where's the Erie Canal?

Where's Niagara Falls?

Where are the Yankees seen

pitching curve balls?

Find Manhattan Island,

home to Wall Street.

Find the Statue of Liberty.

Find hot dogs to eat.

Where's Charlie?

SANTA'S WORKSHOP

North Pole

ADIRONDACK MOUNTAINS

Lake Champlain

Lake Placid

Lake Ontario

Fort Ticonderoga

Niagara Falls

ERIE CANAL

Cooperstown

Albany

HUDSON RIVER "CLEAR WATER" SLOOP AND FESTIVAL

Jamestown

CATSKILL MTS.

Walton
Scarecrow Capital of the World

HUDSON RIVER

MONTAUK LIGHTHOUSE

LUCY-DESI MUSEUM

GUGGENHEIM MUSEUM

FLANDERS DUCK

EMPIRE STATE BUILDING

Long Island

WALL STREET

New York City

YANKEE STADIUM

STATUE OF LIBERTY

Ohio

THE BUCKEYE STATE

Where is Lake Erie?

Where's the boat, *Delta Queen*?

Where are the most pumpkins

that you've ever seen?

Where's a huge rubber stamp?

Where are three halls of fame?

Where's a museum

bearing a cowboy's name?

Where's Charlie?

CEDAR POINT ROLLER COASTER CAPITAL OF THE WORLD

LAKE ERIE

Sanduski

Rock & Roll Hall of Fame

EREE

Cleveland

LARGEST RUBBER STAMP

GOODYEAR

Akron

Goodyear Air Dock

Georges Seurat Topiary Garden

Canton

SCIOTO RIVER

NATIONAL MUSEUM OF USAF

National Pro Football Hall of Fame

Cambridge

Dayton

Columbus

MOTORCYCLE HALL OF FAME

HOPALONG CASSIDY MUSEUM AND FESTIVAL

CHATEAU LA ROCHE

Loveland

CIRCLE VILLAGE

Cincinnati

PUMPKIN FESTIVAL & SHOW

Forked Run State Park

DELTA QUEEN

OHIO RIVER

Pennsylvania

STATE CAPITAL
HARRISBURG

STATE FLAG

DID YOU KNOW...

- The Declaration of Independence was signed in Philadelphia, PA.

- Betsy Ross made the first American flag in Philadelphia, PA.

- The first bubblegum factory was also there, owned by a company called Fleet that still makes bubblegum today.

- The Philadelphia Zoo was the first public zoo in the US.

- Hershey, PA, is the home of the Hershey's chocolate company and is considered the chocolate capital of the United States.

- The American Continental Army spent the winter of 1777–1778 encamped at Valley Forge, PA. Over the course of the winter, a quarter of the troops died from harsh weather and lack of supplies.

Find the Liberty Bell.

Find a ruffed grouse.

At Valley Forge,

find George Washington's house.

Find Gettysburg,

where many men took up arms.

Find Hershey's Kisses.

Find Amish farms.

Where's Charlie?

PRESQUE ISLE LIGHTHOUSE

Lake Erie

U.S.S. NIAGARA

RUFFED GROUSE

POCONO SNAKE FARM

POCONO MOUNTAINS

Erie

PHIL

SELDOM SEEN COAL MINE

BUSHKILL FALLS

Valley Forge

OHIO RIVER

Punxsutawney

THE SLINKY FACTORY

KISS KISS

KISS KISS

KISS KISS

Mars
Pittsburgh

Hollidaysburg

Harrisburg

Hershey

Philadelphia

FRANK LLOYD WRIGHT'S FALLINGWATER

Gettysburg

LIBERTY BELL

AMISH FARM

INDEPENDENCE HALL

Rhode Island

STATE CAPITAL
PROVIDENCE

STATE FLAG

DID YOU KNOW...

● Rhode Island is the smallest state in the U.S.

● 45 Rhode Islands would fit into the state of New York.

● The Newport Jazz Festival, started in 1954, is the world's oldest continually held jazz festival.

● The state bird of Rhode Island is the Rhode Island Red, a chicken with dark red feathers that can lay up to 300 eggs per year.

● The official name of Rhode Island is The State of Rhode Island and Providence Plantations. It is nicknamed "The Ocean State" because every point in the state is within 30 miles of seawater.

● The Providence Athenaeum, America's fourth oldest library, was founded in 1753. One of its most famous members was Edgar Allan Poe.

Where is Block Island?

What's a Rhode Island Red?

Find Pawtucket, the birthplace

of Mr. Potato Head.

Find Providence, Kingston,

Narragansett Bay.

Find Newport,

the place for a jazz holiday.

Where's Charlie?

BLACKSTONE RIVER

ATHENAEUM LIBRARY

EDGAR ALLAN POE

Providence

Pawtucket

HAPPY BIRTHDAY

RHODE ISLAND RED

SEAGRAVE MEMORIAL OBSERVATORY

SCITUATE RESERVOIR

Adamsville

ARCADIA WILDLIFE MANAGEMENT AREA

LEAPFEST INTERNATIONAL PARACHUTE COMPETITION

Kingston

Newport

FLYING HORSE CAROUSEL

Narragansett Bay

ROSECLIFF

BREAKERS

Westerly

MOHEGAN BLUFFS

CLIFF WALK

BEACH WOOD

BLOCK ISLAND

ELMS

TEA HOUSE

Vermont

STATE CAPITAL
MONTPELIER

STATE FLAG

DID YOU KNOW...

- Barre, VT, is considered the "Granite Capital of the World."

- It takes 10 pounds of cow's milk to produce a single pound of cheese. Vermont farmers produce roughly 70 million pounds of cheese each year.

- Vermont granite was used to build the U.S. Supreme Court building in Washington, D.C.

- Ethan Allen organized the Green Mountain Boys in 1770 to fight against Vermont being annexed by New York.

Find the great Quechee Gorge.

See the tall maple trees.

Look for a farm

selling syrup and cheese.

Where's Champ, the sea monster,

stalking the ferry?

Where was Ethan Allen?

Where are Ben and Jerry?

Where's Charlie?

CHAMP the Sea Monster

Lake Champlain

Mt. Mansfield

Lake Memphremagog

Knight's Spider Web Farm

Drive Through a Barn

Burlington

Ethan Allen House

Montpelier

Williamstown

VERMONT TEDDY BEAR

Vermont Teddy Bear Factory

Ben & Jerry's

Killington

Quechee Gorge

Mt. Snow

Maple Syrup Farm

Bennington

Grandma Moses Gallery

CHEDDAR

Now that you've traveled the Northeast with Charlie,
it's time to earn some extra credit.
There's one riddle for each state. Good luck!

Can You Find . . .

a dinosaur park in Connecticut
where footprints are shown . . .

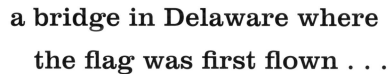

a bridge in Delaware where
the flag was first flown . . .

the world's largest coffee pot
near waterfalls in Maine . . .

a small, red caboose
on a Maryland train . . .

a haunted house in Massachusetts
with a witch and a cat . . .

a groundhog in Pennsylvania
with an umbrella and hat . . .

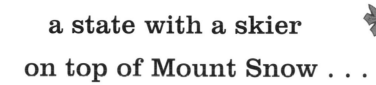

a state with a skier
on top of Mount Snow . . .

a place in New Hampshire
where snowmobiles go . . .

a place in Rhode Island
where folks watch the stars . . .

a state with the first
drive-in movie for cars . . .

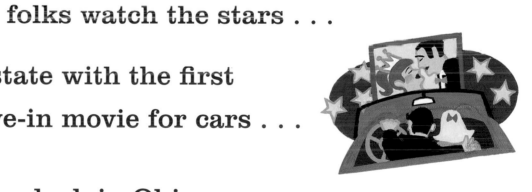

a dock in Ohio
where blimps make a stop . . .

a building in New York
with a gorilla on top?

Good Work!